The Master Swordsman
& The Magic Doorway

The Master Swordsman
& The Magic Doorway

TWO LEGENDS FROM ANCIENT CHINA

Retold and Illustrated by
ALICE PROVENSEN

Simon & Schuster Books for Young Readers

New York   London   Toronto   Sydney   Singapore

For James Paul Mitchell

SIMON & SCHUSTER BOOKS FOR YOUNG READERS
An imprint of Simon & Schuster Children's Publishing Division
1230 Avenue of the Americas, New York, New York 10020
Copyright © 2001 by Alice Provensen
SIMON & SCHUSTER BOOKS FOR YOUNG READERS
is a trademark of Simon & Schuster.
The author gratefully acknowledges the assistance of
Margherita Zanasi, Ma Yue, Dirk Zimmer, and Pei Fin Chin-Kupferman.
The text for this book is set in 17-point Calligraphic 421.
The illustrations are rendered in oil on vellum.
Printed in the United States of America
10 9 8 7 6 5 4 3 2 1

Library of Congress Cataloging-in-Publication Data
The master swordsman and the magic doorway / Alice Provensen
p. cm.
Contents: The master swordsman—The magic doorway
Summary: In two original stories set in ancient China, Little Chu masters the sword,
and Mu Chi escapes death through his marvelous painting.
ISBN 0-689-83232-X
1. Children's stories, American. [1. China—Juvenile fiction. 2. China—Fiction.
3. Short stories.] I. Title.
PZ7.P9457 Tal 2001   [E]—dc21   99-462275

故事

The Master Swordsman

A long time ago,
far away in China,
a group of poor farmers lived in a small village.
All they had in the world were their tumbledown houses,
the clothes they had on their backs,
and a small piece of land.
Each year, when they harvested the rice they had grown,
they hid away enough rice seeds for the next year's planting.

Poor though it was, the village was often set upon by bandits.

The bandit tribe swarmed down the mountain pass to attack the village.
Brandishing their swords, they beat and robbed the people.
"Spare us our miserable scraps," cried the villagers, "or we shall surely starve!"
"You are lucky to escape with your miserable skins!" shouted the
bandit chief. The bandits made off with everything of value they
could find . . . which wasn't much.

"Where can we learn to protect ourselves?" cried Little Chu.
One of the farmers spoke up.

"I have heard of a Master Li living in a distant province," he said. "He is said to be the greatest teacher of the sword in all of China."

"Father, give me permission to go in search of this Master Li," said Little Chu.

"Go, my son, and Good Fortune go with you," said his father.

Little Chu's mother wept bitterly.

After months of wandering, living on a little rice begged from
poor farmers and an occasional stolen onion,
Little Chu was almost ready to give up.

He decided to cross the mountain and look for work in a big city.
On the way, he came to a shabby hut of straw and branches
where a very ragged old man lived, surrounded by
chickens, ducks, a goat, a dog, and ravens cawing on the roof.

Little Chu bowed to the old man. "Reverent Sir, do you know
where I can find Master Li?" he asked.

The old man looked at Little Chu without expression.
"I am called Master Li."

Little Chu got on his knees.
"Will you teach me the sword, Master?"

Master Li said to Little Chu, "I do not teach anymore . . .
but I am getting old and I need someone to help around the place."

"I will help, Sir," said Little Chu.

So it began.

Carrying . . .

Digging . . .

Pitching . . .

Washing . . .

Little Chu slept very soundly.

How heavy the pails!　　　How endless the wood!　　　How far the well!

One day, as Little Chu was carrying water,
a jug came sailing over the hut. BONG!!

"LOOK SHARP!"
glugged the jug.

CRUMP!

"ATTENTION!" clacked the box.

BONK!

"BE ALERT!" creaked the log.

早該知道！

CLUNK!

"ANTICIPATE!" grunted the stewpot.

MASTER LI IS THE MEANEST MAN IN THE WORLD, thought Little Chu,
BUT THE MASTER IS OLD, AND I KNOW HE NEEDS MY HELP.

. . . Two years passed.

One day, without thinking, Little Chu ducked
his head. A big, sharp stone missed him by a hair.

"NOW YOU'RE BEGINNING TO GET IT!"
                                    clicked the stone.

現在你學好了！

ZOOM!

幹得不錯！

"THAT'S THE WAY!"

wheezed the teapot.

"HURRAH!" quacked the ducks.

"GOOD!" crowed the cock.

"SWISH!" went the persimmons and the colander.

NOTHING could touch Little Chu.

One morning, as Little Chu was hard at work, Master Li suddenly drew his great sword.

幹得好！

With a terrific HISS, it spun under Little Chu, who had leaped high in the air.

"WELL DONE, MY SON!" whispered the sword.

The persimmons, the cabbage,   the sword,   the stool,   the colander,

the log,   the pail,   the stewpot,   the rock,

抽刀切菜

the box,   the teapot,   the water jug,   the chair

all applauded Little Chu.

Master Li bowed to Little Chu and said, "You have learned all I can teach you. You are free to go now. Here is the scabbard for your sword. You will never need to draw it. No enemy can touch you."

"USE THE SWORD TO CHOP CABBAGE."

Little Chu returned to his village in triumph. He became the village chef.
The villagers built him a teahouse, and as his reputation as a cook grew,
his family and friends prospered.

Great and important people, and even dangerous people, came from near
and far to watch Little Chu wield his famous sword as he prepared their meals.

No one ever challenged the swordsmanship of Little Chu.

故事

The Magic Doorway

Mu Chi
was the greatest painter
in all of ancient China.
One day he was called to
the court of the emperor.
"Mu Chi, I have a new wall
for you," he said.
"Wait until you see it!
Only you can do it justice."

Mu Chi went to look at the wall.

It was a beautiful wall. . . .

The pure white plaster was as smooth as porcelain.

It stretched without a break, a hole, a window,

or a door to mar it for one hundred feet.

And it was as high as a very tall pine tree.

Mu Chi caught his breath. . . . A wall to dream of!

The emperor, who was watching Mu Chi through

a secret spy hole, clapped his hands.

"I have him!" he said.

So Mu Chi picked up his brushes and began to paint his great picture . . .
a vast landscape of mountains, waterfalls, pine trees,
clouds, wind, and rain.

As he painted, the picture seemed so real, you could walk
into it, and feel the rain on your cheeks, the wind in your hair.

Birds flew through the painting and perched
in the branches that Mu Chi had painted.
The roar of the waterfall filled the palace.

The emperor came to see
the progress of the work.
He clapped his hands!
"It will be the greatest painting
in the world, Mu Chi!"

Greed filled the emperor's
dishonorable heart.
His selfish eyes narrowed.
"You must never paint another
picture," he commanded.

Mu Chi bowed low.
"I will abandon painting when the
picture is finished, Your Imperial
Majesty," said Mu Chi, crossing
his fingers behind his back.

When the emperor was alone with his court, he called his head executioner to him. "It stands to reason an artist will want to continue to paint," he said suspiciously. "Mu Chi cannot be trusted to obey me. He must die the day the picture is finished. We cannot have another picture as fine as this in someone else's palace."

Mu Chi worked for years on the picture.
It grew beneath his hands. His brushes flew . . .
and so did rumors of his fate.

Mu Chi worked long hours in spite of the rumors.
Deer leaped across canyons. Goats played on the rocks.
There were crows cawing in the vast sky.
Rabbits crouched and nibbled the grass.

There were paneled doors that opened onto secret gardens.
There were painted doors opening into charming pagodas,
where one could sit and have tea.
There was a blue door that seemed to go nowhere.

One could walk for hours along the paths of the picture. . . .

And at last it was finished.

The emperor and all his court hurried in stately fashion to the chamber. Only the emperor spoke.
"You have done it, Mu Chi. You have made the greatest picture in the world! But tell me,
where does that little blue door lead?" "Ah, Your Imperial Majesty," said Mu Chi
as the emperor's executioner started toward him, "I will show you."

Mu Chi picked up his brushes and walked up the path to the little blue door. "Farewell, Your Majesty," he said. "I have some more paintings to make, and I cannot make them without a head." Mu Chi opened the door, which led to freedom, and disappeared through it.

The emperor knew that Mu Chi had outwitted him.
He bowed in reverence to the surprising masterpiece of Mu Chi.